The Sled

Written by Carly Crewe

Illustrated by Lisa McKaskell

TORONTO

Dedications

Carly
For Monroe and Faye, for showing me
the world with new eyes and reminding me
to never give up.

Lisa
For my mother, Marie; my stepmother,
Michelle; and all the other women in my
life who pull a sled for me... just in case.

I went for a walk in the snow
the other day

and behind me I pulled a sled.

My children were insistent

they could walk,

that they didn't need the sled.

Still, I pulled it anyway.

Initially, they had **boundless** *energy.*

They ran through the snow,

laughing and **chasing** each other,

and their laughter was musical.

And even though they didn't seem to need it,

I still pulled the sled.

It felt light, and it wasn't hard to pull.

After we walked a bit longer,

one of my girls fell.

She didn't hurt herself,

but she was upset.

She climbed in the sled for a minute...

And I kept pulling.

But she didn't need it for long, and she hopped back out after a short time.

I was happy I had brought the sled
to help her
when she needed a break.

By the later part of the walk they grew tired.

With the fatigue came the emotions,

and the **meltdowns** began.

"Do you want to climb in the sled?" I asked.

They both did.

And I pulled them.

And sometimes we went downhill and it felt easy.

And sometimes we went uphill

and it was *heavy and hard*

and I was *sweating and tired*

And when I was *sweating* and feeling *tired,* almost resentful at the *weight* of them,

I would stop, pause, and breathe.

And sometimes they climbed out,

feeling they didn't need the sled,

and would walk a bit further,

explore a bit more...

But they always returned

to the sled.

And I **always** kept pulling it.

This is what *motherhood* is.

We keep pulling the sled of support.

Even when they don't need it,
we are here to keep them going.

When they do need it, we pull them through.

There are days it feels **light**, and all **downhill**,

and pulling them, **supporting** them, feels

easy.

And there are days when it is all *uphill*.

And pulling them feels so *hard*, and is so

exhausting.

When we are tired from their weight

and from our own fatigue

we pull them.

So Mama,

if your sled feels heavy today,

pause and

take a breath.

You are working hard.

This job is not easy.

There will be days when they won't
need you to pull them,

and it will get *easier*.

You just have to keep pulling the sled.

Carly Crewe

Knows the ups and downs of motherhood well. As a mom to a set of fiery twin girls, Carly enjoys exploring the world through their eyes and learning everyday. Inspired by her own experience of pulling the sled of support for her girls, Carly hopes *The Sled* will support other mothers and remind them that even on the hardest days, you just have to keep pulling the sled.

Lisa McKaskell

Is an illustrator who believes in the value of old-school methods. For an artist and designer who loves doing work with social meaning, *The Sled* was a joy to bring to life. She doesn't have children of her own, but happily pulls the sled of support for her friends and family. She lives for getting messy and jumping in to the next adventure, and is forever loosing pens in her hair and accidentally drinking her paint-water.

First published 2021 by YGTMama Media Co. Press Trade Paperback Edition.

www.ygtmama.com/publishing

ISBN trade paperback: 978-1-989716-29-8

Text copyright: Carly Crewe

Illustration copyright: Elizabeth McKaskell

Printed in China